This book is dedicated

_____

Auntie Always Loves You!

Hello there, little baby, so precious and bright.
You're a bundle of joy, bringing love and delight.

I'm your very proud Auntie—

your built-in dear friend!
Like a mama, but cooler, and there till the end.

When I visit with you, even just for a while,
I'll always be ready with **hugs** and a **smile**.

I've got plenty of love, and it's YOU I **adore!**
There's just so much to give; I've got buckets to pour.

Come on, sweetie pie, let's get ready to play.

We'll have **"Auntie-and-Me"** expeditions all day!

We will play silly games, and we'll laugh the whole time.

I can be the cool auntie: your partner in crime.

I will show you new things. We'll explore many places.
Your checklist of wishes will have no blank spaces.

The entrees we'll cook will get nothing but praise!

We'll read books...Do some crafts...

Visit charming cafes.

You can trust me with **secrets**.
I'll lend you my ear—

understand your perspective
when others won't hear.

And I promise to guide you
with thoughtful advice.

I'll be there when you call me.
No need to ask twice!

Through our laughter and tears—
yes, through thick and through thin—
I'll be your cheerleader whether
you lose or you win!

I will love every moment
and cherish our bond.

I'll support your ambitions,
big dreams,
and beyond.

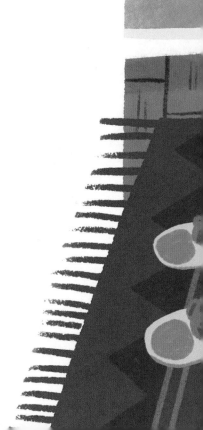

I am not here to judge

when you make a mistake—
through the setbacks
and heartaches and
downturns you take.

Yes, I always will love you

Come rain or come shine.

You can just call me **Auntie**.
The honor's all mine!

For Mina, Leah, Eli, Miles & Claire

About the Author

Katrina Liu is an American-born Chinese/Taiwanese mom and indie author living in San Francisco, CA. She was inspired by her children to create books with Asian-American characters where they can see themselves reflected in. Her mission is to add more Asian representation into the world of children's books and normalize Asian characters in everyday stories. She's also passionate about dual-language learning and has published several bilingual books in Chinese and English for non-native speakers.

ISBN: 979-8-89111-010-6

Check out these other titles by Katrina Liu

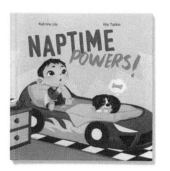

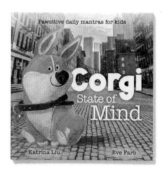

For more books visit
www.lycheepress.com

Made in the USA
Monee, IL
14 December 2024